A Central System Short Story
The Slugs of Dale Cannon
Nicholas Licalsi

STEP INTO THE ROAD

For my grandparents, Roy and Beth, thanks for your encouragement to go outside of procedures and pursue what makes me happy.

Thank You Patrons!

Your generous support has helped me break a few rules here and there and helps me herd my creativity!

Katelyn Combs, Bonnie, BW, Melinda Callender,
Roy & Beth Shockey, Callen McMillian, Sam Meeks, John Middleton.

One

The wooden planks of the living room creaked under the weight of Rystole Whitlock's work boots. Normally he'd have to take them off at the door, a time-consuming process of unlacing the shoes. But there was no time for that.

He was worried he was already too late.

He'd heard the screams from the barn and rushed over with the first tool he could find a pitchfork.

The door had been cracked open, but not busted down with force. It matched all the reports from others who'd experienced the same intrusion.

The wooden stilt house wasn't big, they'd built it just last year, a few kilometers outside of town where the buffcows could roam on the wild prairies of Dale Cannon.

Across from the front door where Rystole stood were the closed doors of two bedrooms. One room Rystole shared with his sisters, the other belonged to his parents.

For months Rystole had lobbied for an extension, a room or area to call his own, if they were still on Feldman's station he'd be getting his own apartment by now. But there was no time on the ranch. That problem never seemed more apparent to Rystole than right now.

The living area had a kitchen and a living room. The living room was to his right, a stone fireplace with shelves built into the wall around it. The room itself was filled with wooden benches and chairs and a short table for board games in the evening.

The kitchen was on the opposite side of the fireplace, it had a horseshoe counter, a small icebox, and a solar-powered range.

The kitchen was where his parents were. The room smelled like his father's vegetable curry and Rystole was reminded the last thing he had was a sandwich during his early lunch period at school.

His parents were in the kitchen. His father, who wore an apron over his collared work shirt and thin khaki pants, was swinging his best cooking knife at the intruders. He seemed out of breath and far from effective.

At least a half dozen slugs, big enough to wrap themselves around Rystole's leg, crawled across the floor of the kitchen and on the wooden counter. Their skin was dark brown like wet dirt and spotted with light brown rings that constantly changed their shape and size like ripples in a puddle.

Despite what others at the town hall meetings had said these weren't the grossest thing Rystole had ever seen. Nonetheless, he wanted them out of his house. Away from his family.

Rystole's mother lay on the ground, unconscious, a giant slug crawled over her exposed arm. She wore the same thing as Rystole, canvas pants, and a short-sleeved shirt.

She'd come inside a few minutes ago, Rystole had promised her he'd take care of docking the tractor and the drones, even though she normally did it.

The obvious thing missing from the room was his siblings.

A few slugs crawled towards the door of the kids' room and Rystole watched the light at the bottom of the door get snuffed out. Proud of his sister's response to the situation he knew she was barricading any small gap the creatures could slip through.

In the lounge room, he twisted the pitchfork in his hand and aimed the slugs headed towards the bedroom.

He stabbed harder than he would if he was moving hay for the buffcows and he sunk the tool into the flesh of the slug. A satisfying thud of the tines hitting the wooden floor meant that the slug was pinned for good.

Except the little slime ball reacted unlike anything Rystole had seen before. The body of the slug separated from the four prongs of the pitchfork making gaping holes in its blobby body.

The holes moved down its body as the slug crawled out from under the fork. Rystole stabbed it again but the slug repeated its reaction quicker than before.

Rystole wasn't stupid, if piercing wouldn't do anything then he'd switch tactics and beat at it with the handle of the tool.

The slug moved slowly across the floor of the lounge room. It didn't dodge the attacks like it did the stabbing and Rystole was putting as much force behind the swing as possible. Breaking the good pitchfork would be a worthwhile price for killing these monsters.

On Rystole's fifth swing the handle buried itself into the slug's body. The slug continued to crawl but Rystole couldn't free the tool from its back. It was as if the pitchfork was a spoon buried in a jar of strawberry jam.

He dropped the weapon as he noticed two more slugs were crawling his way. They'd lost interest in the bedroom and seemed interested in helping their ally. Not that it needed the help.

They backed him into the stone fireplace of the lounge room.

His mother was still lying on the floor, unmoving. She'd suffered the same fate as others who'd been touched by the slugs.

Two slugs were pursuing his father who'd crawled onto the icebox to get the high ground over the slugs but Rystole didn't know what good that would do because one of them was crawling vertically on the freezer's face.

The wall Rystole was backed into had open shelves on either side that stored games, canned food, and various technologies they needed for day-to-day life inside the cabin.

The slugs advanced towards him. They crawled over the short table in the center of the room and the wooden rocking chair his mother often sat in.

Rystole began slinging anything from the shelf he could lay his hands on. A wooden box, filled with board game pieces his father carved, hit the slug on the table. Rystole didn't know or care if it was the same one that'd been stabbed with the pitchfork.

And the slug didn't seem to care much about the box that hit it. The game box opened leaving a mess of pieces scattered on the ground.

Rystole hefted a dense statue his sister made in school at another and missed. The thud shook the cabin's hollow floor.

He slung the family's radio at the converging slugs and immediately regretted his decision. He could have used it to call for help. It wouldn't have saved his own skin but it would have helped his siblings.

But by the time he realized the mistake the radio hit the ground. The metal antenna snapped off with the impact and the plastic body snapped open exposing the inner electronics.

It landed in the center of the group of slugs and there was no way he could retrieve it to call for help. It lay on the ground damaged, but hopefully not beyond repair.

Unexpectedly the slug's approach towards Rystole became chaotic. They weaved away from the radio giving it a wide berth before advancing back on Rystole.

Their change in approach gave him space to grab the broken radio and once it was in his hand again he flipped it on to begin transmitting.

Immediately he heard a deafening shriek like radio static. He realized the device wouldn't do him much good until he reattached the antenna that had busted off.

Looking around to find the antenna he found the shrieking wasn't coming from the radio but the slugs themselves. They were backing away from him.

He approached holding the radio out in front of him like a talisman warding away evil. The slug moved away from him faster than he knew they could.

He had a way of corralling them, and a herd of slugs couldn't be much different from a herd of buffcows.

Two

Rystole stood across the wooden workbench from his friend Bert Morris. The table, like most of the room, was a mess with copious electronics in various states of repair.

A matter printer hummed in the corner and filled the room with the smell of melting plastic and other materials. Racks of electronics used for communication in the colony lined the walls and a few plastic tubs were filled with raw materials. Two desks with embedded terminals sat behind Bert and the workbench.

The room itself was printed concrete, like most of the buildings in town. The walls had the hallmark horizontal lines of piped concrete. The whole town had been printed before the colonists arrived four years ago.

Bert sat in a swivel chair with wheels and was wearing a nice collared shirt that was patched up in a few places. It was the typical clothes of those who worked in the city. Rystole's father wore a similar type of shirt.

The formal wear, at least formal by Rystole's standards, contrasted with his loose-fitting T-shirt and canvas pants. Teachers always pushed him to dress up for class. But Rystole was more interested in saving time when he eventually got back to the ranch.

Bert worked in the town hall and had graduated last cycle despite being the same age as Rystole. The town hall didn't have that many staff members, mainly the town's speaker, doctor, and communication director.

Bert was apprenticing under the comms director. Which is why Rystole had come to him after school with the broken radio and questions about why it repelled the slugs. The same broken radio that was lying in front of his friend on the workbench.

"There's nothing in there that would bother living beings," Bert said, pushing his long sandy hair out of his eyes so he could look at Rystole. "Unless they knew it could be used to call for backup."

"Even if they did know that it's not like an army of pitchfork-wielding ranchers were going to do them any harm," Rystole replied.

Bert nodded his head agreeing with Rystole's point. He poked at the broken radio, eventually popping open the back to get to the inner components.

Rystole learned in school that the radio had two systems of communication. One that enabled them to communicate locally and another one that connected to the tall radio tower in the center of town and connected them with the rest of the Central System.

The wavelengths that the local radio used weren't small enough to cause any tissue damage or irritation like UV or X-rays would, at least not in humans or any other lifeforms humans had discovered or created.

The general theory was any lifeforms able to handle the damaging rays of their local star could stand a few megahertz here or there.

The communication that linked them back to human civilization was another beast entirely. It leveraged submatter pathways that humanity discovered after centuries of research in the stars.

The entire setup was beyond even the comm director's under-standing. The colony of Dale Cannon just needed to know how to install and maintain it. Scientists deep in the Central System figured out the rest.

If something went wrong with Dale Cannon's comms someone monitoring it in the Central System would notice it and send them a new one. But space was big and starships didn't always move quickly enough to save colonies.

"You'd think if the radio irritated them in some way they would avoid the cabins," Bert said after the radio's components were laid out in a neat grid on his desk.

"I wish they would." Rystole wouldn't be worrying about the farm right now if they did.

Bert rolled his chair from the workbench to his desk on the far wall. He typed something into the terminal embedded into his desk as Rystole followed him. Bert was much quicker than Rystole was at using those terminals and a map of the settlement was quickly on the screen.

"Here's where the slugs have attacked," Bert said as several red dots appeared on the screen. "They outline the edge of town. They don't approach the town hall itself."

"That's just because they know it's densely populated and they'd be outnumbered. Right?"

"That's a big assumption, Rye," Bert replied. He rolled across the room on his chair. "We don't know how intelligent they are."

"They can't be that intelligent; there's no civilization on this plan-et," Rystole said.

"That's a very human-centric view of intelligence." Bert began probing the radio with a contraption Rystole hadn't seen before.

"They don't do anything the buffcows don't do, including avoiding large groups of people. The slugs are just more dangerous than the buffs."

"Your cattle aren't exactly harmless," Bert replied still probing at Rystole's broken radio.

Rystole knew he was right. He'd come to school a few times as a kid with bruises and scrapes and a broken arm once.

"As for this thing," Bert continued, "it seems like you busted one of the core stabilizers of the submatter crystal."

Rystole only replied with a confused look now leaning against Bert's desk.

"The stabilizers help integrate your digital inputs with the submatter crystal. Which then sends your data to the tower and out to the Central System."

"So, I broke it?" He didn't need a fancy probe to tell him that.

"You broke it in an interesting way. Knocking out a stabilizer like this increases the output of the crystal. You wouldn't notice it though because most of the radio's interface is digital. It'd just throw errors."

"But a broken stabilizer would make the output stronger?" Rystole said slowly, starting to catch on. "And the stronger signal bothered the slugs?"

It didn't make sense to Rystole, the submatter pathways took millennia to discover and were considered one of humanity's greatest technical achievements.

The slugs on the other hand showed no signs of technological advancement based on the Central System's scan of the planet before Dale Cannon's founding.

There were cases and examples where scans missed signs of life or technology but they were rare. And it was even rarer that those situations ended well for the colonies.

Bert nodded. "And they may be avoiding the town because our radio tower doesn't have the same kind of stabilizers."

"You still use digital inputs to transmit though," Rystole said gesturing to the computer he was leaning on.

"Sure but the tower sends and receives massive packets of information and it's easier to do that with higher outputs from the crystals," Bert responded rolling back to the terminal causing Rystole to jump out of his way.

"So, if we break our stabilizers we could keep the slugs away?" Rystole asked as Bert typed into the terminal.

Rystole was glad to have a potential solution for future attacks but it didn't necessarily help his mother.

"Here it is," Bert said.

His friend had pulled a diagram up on his terminal for Rystole to see. It was a schematic for a submatter radio, but that was all Rystole could tell.

"I thought I'd remembered some research about increasing the output of the crystal," Bert said. "It didn't have any application at the time it was discovered because it wasn't stable enough to transmit data. But I think I could use it to put something together that might help us out."

"Something to keep them away?" Rystole asked.

"Just come back after school tomorrow and I'll show you what I've come up with."

Three

Rystole walked down the dirt path to his home feeling like he'd wasted the day at school and then wasted the afternoon with Bert. He should've skipped class, helped out on the farm, but he needed to see Bert, and showing up at town hall during school hours would've gotten him in trouble.

The teacher spent the whole day going over the complexities of wireless charging.

Rystole'd learned about wireless charging when he was six and the tractor's charging station went out. His mother had pulled him out of school because she needed a second set of hands to help fix it. He didn't do much more than deliver her a wrench or two but she still took the time to show him around the dismantled charger.

Thanks to her he knew about most things in the school's textbook, which was just an in-depth user manual for all the colony's technology. He could pass the senior exam right now but he knew Speaker Grisham wouldn't allow it.

Rystole could hear Grisham saying: "We're a small colony lightyears away from any major system, every citizen needs to know as much as they can about the tools we depend on and the tools that connect us to our fellow humans."

Except when Bert wanted to take the senior exam early and the comms director vouched to take him on as an apprentice Grisham approved it. How repairing radios was more important than raising cattle Rystole still hadn't figured out.

Rystole had about as much connection with the off-world humans as a tractor did with its wireless charging port. He knew they were out there, somewhere in the stars. He knew they helped him survive because they sent resupply packages every two and a half years. But there was nothing that made them tangible or important to his day-to-day life.

The colony of Dale Cannon was nearly self-sufficient and on the path to abundance and if the off-worlders quit sending them supplies Rystole had no doubt they'd find a way to survive.

Of course, that wasn't the plan.

The plan was: once Dale Cannon was an abundant colony more settlers would arrive and work to turn the planet into the Central System's newest and furthest colony in the stars.

The colony's population would grow tenfold overnight and new specialists would arrive and so would new technology.

There'd be no expectation for a student to study the colony's user manual because it would hold only a small fraction of the things available to them.

If Speaker Grisham had his way the infusion of new specialists would arrive tomorrow. Realistically, Rystole expected any kids he had to be learning from the specialists, not working a farm like him.

Of course, the slugs would keep that from happening if they kept raiding farm cabins and putting the inhabitants in comas. His mother wasn't the first to fall prey to the attacks.

Usually, whole families would be wiped out only to be found a day or two later when no one heard from them.

Everyone kept saying the Whitlocks were lucky that only his mom was touched by the slugs. But all Rystole could think about was the list of chores that would be difficult or impossible without his mom around.

As he walked up to the house he saw his oldest sister and father, who still wore his thin work pants, struggling to manually herd the buffcows in the distance. Rystole used his hand terminal he summoned a few herding drones from the barn as he went to lend a hand.

Juniper, his sister, made a disgusted face as she saw the bots fly up.

"We don't need those," she protested.

"You do if we want a decent harvest next month." Rystole pointed to a small group of furry buffcows headed off to a pasture of barley. Thinking about doing a harvest without his mom was gut-wrenching but he focused on the task at hand.

The drones let out a low hum that encouraged the cattle to move away from the crops. Rystole and his family corralled the group in through the gate and his sister swung the gate closed, having to jump on it because the gate was so heavy. She usually smiled at the fun ride but today her face was as plain as if she was drying dishes.

"What took you so long to get home?" His father asked as they finished up other chores around the farm. His father wasn't scolding, it sounded more like a professional interest.

Rystole explained his visit to Bert at a high level and got the low down on how his father's day went. His mother did most of the work on the farm while Rystole and his sister were at school and his father was at work in town.

Like every colonist, his father knew the gist of running a farm but his mother had a certain knack for it while his father often said, "It takes a special kind of person to do that work and your mom's the most special person I know."

They ate the dinner Leilani, his youngest sister, prepared together at the dinner table ignoring the empty place that was set out of habit.

"We could have gotten the buffs in without the drones," Juniper said, not one to put a tool down before the job was overdone. "It's more natural that way, and it's how ancient cowboys used to do it."

"Ancient cowboys weren't herding genetically spliced cows," Rystole said. "You know what else is natural? Broken bones and concussions."

"He's right, June, we should have used them from the start," their father said.

"Mom doesn't use them," Juniper whined. But seemed to regret the statement after she said it.

"She does. When she needs to," Rystole said. "If you and I weren't there she'd use them. And I remember when she was pregnant with Leilani and Harry she used them." Those were the early days of the colony when they still lived in town and it was a treat to explore past the colony's tall printed walls.

"That was just because you were too young to help," Juniper retorted.

"Harry was born two summers ago," Rystole said, gesturing at his little brother who was being fed by his father.

"I'm just calling it how I see it," she said sticking her tongue out.

The comment hit him harder than it should have. It was a phrase June picked up from their mom.

"Rye is right," his father said as Harry chewed up his spoonful of mashed potatoes. "We don't get extra credits by doing things the old-fashioned way. We need to use the tools at our disposal, even if I can't get them to work right half the time."

The rest of the dinner went on and Leilani, barely four, babbled on about what she'd learned in school. The family cleaned the dishes.

After Harry and Leilani were put to bed then the three of them played a board game and hid the fourth set of pieces in the box trying to collectively ignore that the cabin was missing someone. Juniper won the game and wouldn't let anyone live it down as she trotted off to bed.

"You want a beer?" Rystole's father asked pulling one out of the cold side of the deep freeze.

"I'm fine," Rystole said, he'd never liked the taste. Plus as a teenager, he felt the only appeal of drinking was getting away with it while your parents weren't watching.

"I talked to Dr. Yu today."

"Yeah?"

"Yeah," his father replied.

"Anything..." Rystole didn't know the words he was supposed to say next.

"Nothing new," his father said after a sip of his drink.

Rystole flipped through the book that was in his lap but didn't really read any of the words on the page.

"She's stable at least," his father said after some silence, "like the rest of them."

"Mr. Montgomery is still doing okay?" Rystole asked.

Morton Montgomery was the first person to be attacked by the slugs months ago. Rystole knew of him, the colony was small enough for that, but everyone's interest in him peaked when he was attacked.

"As far as Dr. Yu can tell he is. He's still losing weight though..."

"He had some to spare," Rystole responded.

His father gave him a look indicating his comment was rude and unuseful. "I don't want you doing anything stupid with Bert. You and him are smart kids, smart enough to get yourselves into trouble you can't get out of."

"We're not doing anything dangerous." Rystole didn't think this was a lie, mostly because he didn't know what Bert was planning to do.

"I still remember when you broke your arm trying to break the buff-bull that charged mom." His dad said it with a smile, but Rystole saw that there was concern in his eyes. "You weren't much older than June."

"At least I had the sense to use an electric harness."

"An electric harness for an adult," his father said with a chuckle. "It was two sizes too big for you!"

"It could've worked," Rystole said. It was the phrase he'd always fallen back on even though everyone in the room knew it wasn't true.

"Then you wandered in here holding your arm saying you thought something was wrong with it." His dad shook his head in disbelief. "I was still nursing your mom from the charge."

"Well, I was right that there was something wrong with it." The memory, though painful, brought a smile to his face.

"Just be safe kid, we're not going to be able to get much done if something happens to you too."

"I'll be fine," Rystole said, but he was worried the statement was already a lie.

Four

The school day couldn't pass by quickly enough for Rystole and he was eager to see what Bert was working on. He wandered into the town hall seeing himself to Bert's office which was more of a workshop or unkempt mess depending on who you asked.

It matched Bert's current appearance. His long sandy hair was slicked back and gleamed with oily grease. His shirt, still the patched collared one from yesterday, now had more wrinkles and the topmost button undone.

"What have you got for me?" Rystole asked as walked into the room.

Bert was startled by the interruption and he jumped at his workbench knocking over a few items sitting nearby.

"Are you cutting class for this? You should still be in school," Bert jested talking like an adult despite being the same age as Rystole.

"Check your terminal. I've been out of school for a few minutes."

Bert cursed under his breath. "I thought I had more time."

"At least tell me what you're doing," Rystole said. He looked over Bert's shoulder at the project.

The device Bert was working on seemed to have the same components as the radio, just not in the same position and with a few other circuits added in. The shape was unsettlingly familiar to Rystole.

"It's a…" Bert paused for a minute to think of the right word.

"It's a gun," Rystole pointed out in shock.

"Well not exactly," Bert said in his defense.

Both the boys had grown up as friends on Feldman's station, a bond that linked them even though their interests and personalities differed. Feldman's station was a large, but still cramped, space station deep inside of the Central System.

There wasn't enough room there for Bert and Rystole's parents so they decided to try their hand a colonizing a new planet. It was a common story among Dale Cannon's colonists—and colonists throughout the Central System.

Guns could be printed on the matter printer that hummed away in the corner of Bert's workshop. But having a gun on Feldman's would've been considered a crime.

Not only could a gun hurt others but more importantly it could damage the delicate station that millions of people lived on.

Most people in the colony, including Rystole, still held that association in their minds. Which is why even if it became necessary for the residents of Dale Cannon to arm themselves against wildlife, pirates, or other threats, Rystole doubted many people would be able or willing to take up arms. And Rystole was pretty sure he'd include himself in that group.

Despite multiple attacks from slugs no one had been willing to publicly request a firearm at any of Dale Cannon's town hall meetings.

Not that Rystole thought shooting the slugs would do much more good than stabbing them with a pitchfork.

"That's the barrel, there's the trigger and the handle," Rystole said while pointing at Bert's device. It had the distinct L shape that Rystole had seen in the few action movies he'd watched.

"It doesn't shoot projectiles so I wouldn't consider it a gun," Bert continued.

There were standard designs for a lot of the colony's equipment including a few designs for guns. If Bert had used one of those designs on the matter printer Speaker Grisham would be notified. And designing one without the use of the standard file would look like Bert was going behind the speaker's back.

"If it looks like a ducken, quacks like a ducken, but can't fly like a ducken—" Rystole started.

"Fine it's a gun," Bert relented. "But it won't actually hurt any humans. It should only affect the slugs."

Bert then went into explaining the gun in far more detail than Rystole needed. The broad strokes that Rystole understood were that Bert had used the research paper's amplification circuit on the submatter crystal and enabled that amplification through a trigger circuit.

"Does it work?" Rystole asked, cutting to the chase.

"Well, not yet I need to integrate one or two more things. And once it's done being wired we won't actually know if it affects the slugs. Like I can probe the output and know if it's running hot but won't know if this is really what the slugs were fleeing."

Rystole smiled a devilish grin. "We can figure that out easy enough."

"I don't like where you're going with this."

"It's simple. When you're done we'll just go looking for a slug or two. Hit 'em with this. See if it works."

"No one knows where the slugs are."

"But there are reports of them being spotted on the outskirts of the farms."

"It's not a guarantee. And what happens if we do find them and they touch you? I can't carry your coma'd ass back to town." Bert eyed Rystole who was significantly taller than Bert and mostly muscle from working on the farm.

"It'll be fine. We'll stay out in the open. We can run if we need to. They only get people because they're cornered in their house."

"Montgomery was in his field."

"Montgomery couldn't outrun a log cabin. Besides, we'll have the gun."

"A gun that might fire blanks," Bert protested weakly.

Rystole was a hound with a bone. He looked at his friend, determined to get his way. A familiar gaze that always seemed to convince Bert to see things his way.

"Come back tonight," Bert said with resignation. "I'll have the thing done then."

***

Rystole returned after what felt like a grueling evening of wrapping up chores on the farm and fixing his father and sister's mistakes they'd made without his mother there. Dinner was quick and he excused himself after little Harry was put to bed and the cabin had been cleaned up.

The whole family had a bit of a gloomy mood about them, for obvious reasons, and Rystole, while he shared their feelings, didn't enjoy lingering in them.

He had hope: Bert's gun. Their ability to kill or capture some slugs could be the breakthrough that would bring his mother back to the farm and solve the family's problems.

Rystole returned to Bert's lab at the town hall having to tap on the window to be let in since the place was locked after hours.

Always a poor judge of time, Bert informed Rystole that it wasn't quite done yet but it was close and would be ready shortly. Rystole took a seat on one of the wooden benches in the town hall's hallway.

Bert shook Rystole awake excitedly, "I've got it working!"

Rystole's back was sore from falling asleep on the hard bench but he soon matched his friend's excitement. Bert showed him several tests that he'd run to prove to him it worked but Rystole was only interested in one thing.

"Let's go find a slug," he said.

"It's the middle of the night."

Rystole shrugged. "Take a caffeine pill. If we come back with a slug I'm sure Speaker Grisham will give you the day off tomorrow."

"Yu is actually my boss."

"Then I'll give you the day off."

Bert groaned as if Rystole had told that joke a dozen times, which he had. Despite Bert's reservations eventually Rystole dragged him out of the town hall.

They lit their way with a few headlamps and Rystole carried an emergency kit backpack they found in one of the supply rooms.

Leaving the tall printed concrete walls of the town undetected was easy. The gates opened for Rystole since his family's cabin was outside of the town walls.

Instead of taking the familiar path home Rystole led them down another led away from the town. When it was clear it would dead end into the land of the Tormund family Rystole stepped off the road and into the overgrown plants and forest.

Bert groaned the whole time. He pointed out he only had thin-soled shoes and he could feel every rock underfoot and thorn that grazed his legs.

Rystole, who was always wearing heavy work boots, suggested that his friend should avoid stepping on things that would hurt him.

The evening was cool and dry the long summer days were coming to an end. Rystole knew the cold air meant fall thunderstorms would be visiting soon.

The chirping of bugs and wind in the leaves startled to the boys since any sound could have been a slug. They didn't know if the slugs climbed trees and when there branches above them rustled Rystole shot the gun in that direction just to be safe.

After the third time, Bert told him to stop and mumbled something about battery life.

The moons were high in the sky by the time they found a specimen and it seemed to be crawling along eating the leaves and the grass.

As soon as Rystole spotted the mud-brown slug with its light brown rings rippling on its back. Rystole pointed the beast out Bert who immediately began to panic.

"What if there are more? Don't these things travel in packs?" Bert asked with a hoarse whisper.

Rystole shrugged his shoulders. "Just keep a lookout," he whispered in response.

He leveled the gun at the slug and pulled the trigger but the slug didn't explode into pieces or flop over onto its back. Rystole realized he didn't know what he'd expected to happen.

"Did it look like it shivered to you?" he asked Bert.

"Is that a slug over there?" Bert pointed.

Rystole didn't look in the direction Bert indicated. He was busy checking the gun's battery level.

"No it's just a knot on a tree," Bert answered his own question.

Rystole crept forward getting closer to the slug trying to step quietly through the grassy plain. It wasn't easy for him in his thick boots.

He pointed the gun at the slug again and pulled the trigger. The gun made no sound and neither did the slug. Rystole held the trigger down letting the radio run longer.

Suddenly the circle patterns on the slug's skin seemed to vibrate becoming looping wave patterns. Then as quickly as it began the patterns froze in their chaotic shape and the slug quit chewing on the grass in front of it.

"We did it!" Rystole shouted and was immediately hushed by his friend. Rystole approached the slug reaching out to poke it.

"Stop!" Bert shouted. The cry echoed through the quiet night and could probably be heard for kilometers, not that there was anyone this far out of town to hear it.

"What if it's still toxic?" Bert asked.

Rystole grabbed a nearby stick and poked the slug with it instead. Nothing happened.

"It's dead," Rystole said.

"There is no way you possibly know that."

"It's not moving."

"Your mom's not moving but she's not dead," Bert stated factually. "Sorry, that came out harsh."

"No, you're right." Rystole slung the emergency pack off his back and rummaged around for a blanket or rope.

He was lucky enough to find a few feet of cordage and a thick synwool blanket. Carefully the boys wrapped up the slug and carried it back to town in the backpack.

Bert cursed the whole way back between yawns while Rystole hefted the slug-laden pack ecstatic about the successful hunt they'd just completed.

Finally, the colonists of Dale Cannon had a way to fight back.

Five

The boys woke up to the sound of Dr. Yu unlocking the door to his office. They'd each fallen asleep on one of the wooden waiting benches in the concrete hallway of the town hall.

They'd gotten back so early in the morning that it didn't make sense for Rystole to go home. Especially since he wanted to come back first thing. Worried he'd miss something important.

The hospital wing of the town hall was big, but not nearly big enough now that people were being attacked by the slugs. Two of the patient rooms were overfilled with a half dozen people each. All of them on life monitoring equipment. Rystole's mother being one of them.

Dr. Yu was clearly startled to see the boys. He likely feared the worst. Rystole tried to relax him, saying that everything was more than fine.

Rystole followed the doctor into the office. Bert lagged behind his greasy hair a mess from sleeping on the uncomfortable benches.

Dr. Yu's office was smaller than Bert's lab and significantly cleaner. A large wooden desk sat in the middle of the room with a radio sitting on the corner of it. The desktop was polished and looked as good, if not better, than the furniture Rystole's father had carved for the house.

Wood was plentiful on this planet, and a lot of the residents considered themselves lucky to be able to use and work with it considering they'd grown up in the metal hallways of Feldman's station. Yu seemed to be no exception to this.

Another desk sat behind the high-backed swivel chair that Yu took a seat in. That desk was the typical plastic kind that held an embedded terminal inside of it. It was the kind of easy-to-print model that filled Rystole's school room.

A few wooden shelves held medical supplies. These were assembled with less care than the desk made out of necessity. A wooden coat rack, still rough and unsanded, held the white coat that Yu usually wore. Right now he had a knitted sweater pulled over a collared shirt and thin khaki pants.

There were two chairs in front of the desk, again plastic pre-designed models, and the doctor gestured for them to take a seat.

Rystole ignored the suggestion.

"What can I help you boys with?" Dr. Yu asked. His early morning voice was deeper than Rystole remembered hearing at the town hall meetings.

Rystole placed the backpack down on the wooden table. He slid the synwool-covered slug out and cut the cordage with the folding knife he kept in his pocket for chores around the farm.

"Be careful with that," Bert said looming next to Rystole.

Rystole wasn't worried and soon the blanket fell off of the slug.

The doctor gasped and stood up from his chair pointing to the door. He told the boys to escape. He reached for the radio on his desk to call for help.

"I'm pretty sure it's dead, or at least incapacitated," Rystole said giving the blanket a shake. It jiggled the slug a little but the beast didn't move or fight back.

The blanket was cool to the touch and had a dampness about it that made Rystole uneasy.

He wiped his hand on his thick pants as he sat back in the plastic chair in front of the doctor's desk.

"We were hoping you would take a look at it for us," Bert asked meekly. Either from this being an interaction with his boss, or the early morning, Rystole wasn't sure.

It took Dr. Yu a little bit of time to grow comfortable with the situation. He paced back and forth behind the desk hesitant to take a seat in case the slug came back to life.

As he paced back and forth he questioned the boys about how they came across a slug let alone brought it back here.

Rystole told the story, doing his best not to describe the device they used as a gun to avoid freaking out the doctor more. He made the whole thing sound simpler than it was, leaving out how far out of town they had to walk and how late they got back.

Bert wanted to fill in the details of how the device worked but it was clear Yu was less than interested in those details.

Finally, Yu stopped his pacing and stood over the slug on his desk.

"You two should get some rest," the doctor said. "I'll take this to the operating room, dissect it, and record my notes. When you come back this afternoon I'll give you an update. Rys, I'll let your teacher know you won't be at school because you were working on something for me. Bert, I guess I'll give you the day off."

"See I told you so," Rystole commented to Bert with a sly grin.

"Does your father know where you are?" The doctor asked.

"I told him I was coming into town to hang out with Bert for the evening."

"You two are damn lucky this worked out," the doctor said without an ounce of pride in his voice. "If you ever get the idea to do something like this again at least keep an adult in the loop."

Rystole gestured at Bert, who by the standards of the colony was effectively an adult.

"You know what I mean," Dr. Yu said cutting Rystole's protests off before they could start.

Rystole rolled his eyes and left. Arguing with the double standards of adults would be as difficult as arguing with Juniper. The pair napped at Bert's house, took much-needed showers, and returned as soon as they could.

When the boys returned to the operating room they found Yu in a bright yellow hazmat suit leaning over a metal table with the slug on it. The doctor looked like he was prepared to take a spacewalk.

It was certainly more gear than Rystole expected considering he'd captured the slug in nothing more than pants and an old t-shirt.

The doctor's paranoia looked ridiculous even if it was justified. But Rystole knew if the colony's doctor was paralyzed there'd be a steep learning curve for the next person who took his place.

The boys were able to look into the operation room through a glass window. The room they waited in had a sink built into the wall but no seats.

A terminal was embedded in the wall and Bert read off Yu's dictation notes as they came through.

There weren't any earth-shattering discoveries documented in the notes, and most of them were just Yu's theories on how things might work based on other biological structures he'd studied.

"Did you figure anything out?" Rystole asked as the doctor shed the protective gear he wore.

"Only that they have more in common with a rodent than bugs," Yu replied as he pulled off his mask. "And even that would be a liberal classification."

"Is there anything that you found that could help my mother? And the others who were attacked?"

Dr. Yu's expression wasn't encouraging. "I found a few glands that I think might have the toxin in them. I'll need to do more analysis though."

"It's a real shame this one was dead," Yu continued. The remark was contemplative, like when Rystole's mother talked about what she wanted the buffcows to do even though they couldn't understand her. "If it was alive I could have studied a lot more about how the inner workings work."

"Bringing it back if it was alive wouldn't have been easy," Bert said.

"No, no, you're right," the doctor said. "I'm impressed you boys have brought back as much as you did."

Rystole beamed with pride.

The doctor saw the smile. "However," he added, "I'm certainly not encouraging you to go on another hunting expedition."

"What if we made the device a little less powerful?" Rystole asked Bert. "Just powerful enough to stun it."

His friend gave him an uneasy look.

"I'm not really interested in getting in the business of weapons manufacturing," Bert said. "I did this because it was an interesting project. I didn't think it'd work. Or that we'd use it."

"Nonetheless, we're going to want to document your design and send it off to the Central System so they can refine it and make more of them," the doctor said.

"And how long will that take?" Rystole asked rhetorically. "There are people, families, being hurt here and now. You could have another four people crammed into your infirmary tonight."

"I don't like it any more than you do," the doctor said half-heartedly. "But this is the protocol and it's what we need to do."

Rystole rolled his eyes.

Who knew how many more slugs would attack as they waited for the Central System to take action?

The Central System might send a weapon design to be printed. More likely they would send scientists and military experts to assess the threat. Who knew how it would hamper Dale Cannon's ability to become a full-on settlement and trading center like it planned to be.

Not to mention there was a chance that the Central System abandoned the planet altogether, Rystole'd heard stories of them doing that if there was a sign that humans couldn't inhabit the planet one way or another.

He'd spend years on Feldman's station, cramped into a one-bedroom apartment with his parents. Central System was committed to providing housing for everyone, but it wasn't good housing. Not the spacious two-bedroom cabin his family built together.

When he saw Dale Cannon from space all he could see was freedom. He wasn't interested in waiting ten or fifteen years waiting to apply for another colony mission.

"I need to talk with Grisham about this," the doctor said cutting Rystole's thoughts short. "And we'll see if we can present it at the weekly town hall meeting tonight. Bert, you should start documenting things because I suspect Grisham is going to want to get this out as soon as possible."

Bert nodded in agreement.

"Rys, go see your family and make sure you're back here by tonight," the doctor said. "Grisham and I are going to want to give you two our appreciation at the meeting, so wear something nice."

"What about finding a cure for my mom and everyone else?" Rystole asked.

"Trust me it's my top priority," Dr. Yu said. "But I suspect there will be a lot of long nights ahead of me figuring that out. I want those folks cured and awake as soon as anyone else. Doesn't speak to my abilities as a doctor to have a sick bay full of comatose people."

Rystole had no doubt the doctor wanted his mom cured, but he could think of a few people who wanted it more, himself included.

Six

The town hall meeting was held in the auditorium of the town hall building and the room was about as empty as usual. Even if the entire town showed up the room would only be half full at most.

The stage was made of raw wooden boards that creaked as people walked across the stage. There were stairs on each side of the stage that led down into the seating area.

The seats themselves were printed plastic, as hard and comfortable as rocks. They closed up like a clam if you stood up, often making a loud snapping sound.

The whole room had been put together in a week or less. It was a priority for Speaker Grisham to have a meeting place for the town. So he pushed to have the project done as soon as the colony landed. Everyone pitched in, even if they had their own houses to build and furnish, but once it was good enough, the citizens of Dale Cannon moved on to the real priorities.

Despite this, Grisham often insisted that the town hall's auditorium would eventually be considered a historic place, maybe even a playhouse. Somewhere visitors would remember the original colonists that made the trading hub possible.

Rystole thought those people, even if some were his ancestors, were as far away and meaningless as the off-world citizens of the Central System.

Speaker Grisham walked onto the stage and stood behind a plastic podium that had been printed early on as well. Despite the intricate decorative designs printed onto its front the podium still looked cheap. But Grisham hadn't bothered to make a nicer one out of wood.

Rystole sat close to the stage. His sisters and father were to his right. Harry sat in his father's lap playing with a plastic key chain. Bert was on his left, his parents next to him.

Normally Rystole would sneak in late and sit in the back or skip the meeting altogether. Tonight he sat close to the stage awaiting his recognition for catching a slug.

Grisham, with his neatly combed mustache and long brown hair with streaks of grey in it, read over the meeting's agenda. It had the same boring things on it about production values, weather predictions, and updates from the Central System. All of them were accessible through a radio or hand terminal.

But the meeting covered these items thanks to tradition. Grisham was a sucker for traditions.

Rystole tried not to doze off during those rote announcements. He was exhausted, and despite the plastic auditorium seat being uncomfortable he felt like he could nap anywhere.

Then the speaker got to the announcement portion of the meeting, where Rystole and his friend would be mentioned.

"We are all aware of the havoc the brown-ringed slugs have brought to this community," Grisham said in his most official tone of voice. "Nearly a dozen farms have been attacked and I've been working constantly with the Central System to look into what can be done to resolve this issue"

Rystole had heard Grisham use that line in every town meeting since the first attack but had yet to see any fruit from the comment.

"As announced in the previous four town hall meetings the Central System has agreed to send a minister, who is in transit. Additional officials are traveling on the same ship. Those *professionals* will help us resolve this issue. They will be here in two to three weeks' time."

Grisham softly cleared his throat before continuing.

"Which is why it's disappointing to hear that some of our younger citizens have decided to take the matter into their own hands and attacked a creature in the wild."

Rystole checked the nice collared shirt he'd put on to make sure it was lying flat. He did not doubt that if this auditorium became a historical place, a picture from this night would be hanging on the walls.

Unfortunately, the shirt itself was littered with wrinkles and covered in patches. He'd truthfully only worn it twice and finally found it this evening in the bottom of his dresser drawer.

"I want to make it clear that neither the Central System nor I condone this kind of behavior," Speaker Grisham said. "The slugs have been identified as a semi-critical threat to the colony and the only reason we haven't abandoned the colony yet is because victims are still alive.

"If things get worse, and we believe they could if we continue to antagonize them, then the abandonment of this colony will be imminent and that would be a waste of all our hard work."

"There's no way he knows that for sure," Bert whispered to Rystole.

"This is buff turds," Rystole said.

"He's implying that they're intelligent in some way," Bert continued. "He and his superiors might know something we don't."

"I would like to propose a mandatory curfew," Grisham continued. "For everyone's protection. Cabins outside the town are welcome to shelter within the town walls if desired. Hopefully, the Central System and I can come up with a solution soon and this curfew will become unnecessary."

Bert raised his hand shouting out the question before the speaker acknowledged him. "You say if we antagonize them this could get worse, are you implying that the slugs are intelligent?"

"At this time, we have no—" the speaker began but was cut off by the scream of a man in the audience.

"Turn on the lights!" a woman shouted.

"Slugs!" another audience member shouted as the entire auditorium erupted in panic.

Rystole and Bert looked behind them. They were sitting, with their families, near the front of the auditorium, expecting to be on stage shortly. From the chaotic movement of the crowd, the slugs seemed to be invading from the back.

Rystole's father lifted Harry and his youngest sister onto the stage gesturing at an emergency exit. Juniper climbed up on her own leading her sister, likely in the same way she had when the slugs invaded the house so recently.

The speaker was still using the microphone now directing people to use the emergency fire exits but the lights still hadn't come up in the auditorium.

Bert began climbing up on the stage but Rystole grabbed his sleeve.

"The gun. Let's use it," Rystole said.

"Grisham just said we shouldn't." Bert's face protested longing for the exit.

"Grisham would tell us not to herd buffcows if that's what the Central System told him to do," Rystole said.

There were at least two people in the audience who were still in their seats. The only excuse for that was that the slugs already got them.

"They're attacking us," Rystole said. "We're not hunting or antagonizing them."

It was clear that this line of logic wouldn't convince Bert.

"Just give me your keycard. I'll do it myself." Rystole was determined to do something and did little to hide it on his face.

"No, no, I'll go," Bert relented.

Rystole and Bert dipped through the backstage hallway that exited near the offices. Rystole kept checking over his shoulder but the slugs weren't quick enough to keep up with them.

They barged into Bert's office and Rystole immediately realized the reason he couldn't have gone alone.

"You took it apart!?"

Seven

The gun was in pieces on Bert's workbench. A few probes were hooked up to it their wires trailing into a monitor. It was hard for Rystole to tell what were tools and what belonged in the contraption.

Bert looked as frazzled as Rystole. He clutched at words to explain himself. Rystole gathered enough to understand this was part of the process of sending the designs back to the Central System.

Rystole checked the hallway as his friend rushed to reassemble the gun. A dozen Slugs had begun to head down the hallway from both directions and soon there wouldn't be any way to escape short of breaking the small windows on the workshop's exterior wall.

It was a better plan than dying but they'd catch hell from Grisham for not fleeing when they had the chance and damaging town property in the process. Rystole began searching the room for materials that could be used against the slugs.

A weapon wouldn't be useful. He'd seen firsthand that any kind of physical damage was useless. Bert was repairing the only thing they knew of that could harm them.

The room was filled with dismantled technology but none of it was farm equipment so Rystole was out of his element.

"Why do you think they're attacking town hall right now?" he asked Bert.

Bert was too focused on the repairs to respond.

"They could be attacking because we are all here in one place," Rystole continued. "But we've been meeting like this every week since we settled the colony."

"It's the slug we killed," Bert said dismissively. "Grisham was right. we antagonized them."

Rystole didn't love the idea of Grisham being right. Mostly because it meant that waiting for the Central System's minister to arrive was the best move. And that felt like the slowest.

"How would they know it's us? Shouldn't there be other predators on Dale Cannon?"

"Try this," Bert said, shoving the gun into Rystole's hand.

Rystole peeked his head out the door and saw the slugs advancing, with even more behind them. There were at least two dozen now. More than he'd seen at any given time. More than he'd ever heard appear in any attack.

The slugs didn't quite fill the width of the hallway. But walking through it without touching one would be harder than avoiding buff manure in the herd's pasture.

Rystole aimed at the closest one and pulled the trigger.

Nothing happened.

He pulled the trigger and held it, remembering that on his first hunt, the gun took some time to take effect.

The slugs grew closer. The gun was having no effect. Rystole ducked back into the lab.

"No good," he said, giving the gun back to Bert.

Rystole's eyes began to dart around the room looking for something to put over the air gap under the door. It was the most effective protection according to Grisham's reports in previous town hall meetings.

Rystole spotted a flimsy box on one of the shelves and dumped out the contents.

"What are you doing?" Bert shouted. "That could have been expensive!"

Rystole ripped the box open laying it flat against the door and the floor. "Do you have tape?"

"Second toolbox, three drawers down," he said, his face still buried in the gun.

"Not there," Rystole said, starting a drawer full of hammers. He grabbed one with a large metal head just in case he needed to break a window.

"Sorry, third from the right, second from the left."

Rystole pulled the drawer open and found every kind of tape he could imagine. He grabbed the cargo tape and began to tape the ripped box to the door.

"Here. Try this," Bert said.

"Is it going to work this time?" Rystole asked as he grabbed the gun.

"I could test it but that'd take time."

Rystole poked his head and arm out the door. The slugs were just over a meter from the door. He pointed the gun and held the trigger down. The light brown rings on the back of a slug made a familiar wave pattern.

Then the wave pattern stopped. The slug started crawling towards him again and he retreated back into the workshop.

"Nothing?" Bert said with a worried look on his face.

"Nothing useful."

Rystole tapped the box to the floor closing the gap. He ran tape around the edges unsure of how thin of a gap the slugs needed.

The box covering the door's gap rustled. The tape strained to hold onto the door but didn't quite break free.

This pattern repeated slowly dying down in frequency but neither Rystole nor his friend wanted to venture out of the safe lab.

So boys waited for what felt like forever. Every single sound from the creak of pipes, to the settling of junk, startled them.

Bert continued to work on the gun but even Rystole could tell the work was unfocused and chaotic.

An unusual sound startled them. Rystole realized it was people talking in the hallway.

There was some shouting of coordination but Rystole couldn't make out what was being said. Then a loud crashing sound rang out.

It startled both of them. But not as much as the knock on the door that followed.

"Rye, Bert, are y'all in here?" It was the voice of Rystole's father.

Rystole pushed the door open, ripping the tape off the floor, almost hitting his father in the face.

Rystole let out his breath and hadn't even noticed he was holding in and hugged his father. A half dozen people, mostly ranchers, were in the hallway. Bert found his mother and hugged her, glad to be alive.

"What the hell were you thinking?" his father asked after they finished their embrace. "I was worried sick. When we didn't find your body in the auditorium I couldn't even begin to imagine what had happened."

Rystole noticed a large plastic box in the middle of the hallway and some of the group gathered around it arguing about what to do next.

"What's in the box?" Rystole asked.

"A slug," his father said.

Rystole wasn't sure if he was serious or not but looking at his face he realized he was.

"We caught one?" Rystole asked.

"More of we kept it from being able to do anyone else harm," his father said. "When we came down the hall it was just crawling in a circle like a tractor missing a wheel."

"When I poked my head out there was a whole army of them," Rystole said. "I blocked the door like we're supposed to but I still thought they'd get in."

"Well it seems like they decided to leave," his father said. "We tried to attack them but it wasn't much use, eventually we just retreated to a house and blocked the gaps of the doors and windows. We watched through the windows and saw them leave, then came to find out what had happened."

Rystole noticed Speaker Grisham round the corner. He hadn't originally been in the group that caught the slug but did come out now that the risk had been neutralized.

The Speaker addressed the boys and their families. "I'm glad neither of you were hurt but you should have evacuated like the rest of the town. What possessed you to hide in an office?"

Bert stayed silent. Not eager to explain himself. So Rystole spoke up.

"We have the gun here, we wanted to test it, but it wasn't working." He then put two and two together and was about to add something but the speaker cut him off.

"This is the most preposterous thing I've heard. You hunt one down as a fluke and think you're a Central System commando. We're just lucky you're okay. Dr. Yu is running out of beds in his infirmary with this last attack.

"Bert you have a very clever head on your shoulders and the Central System needs a copy of your plans as soon as possible. And Rystole," Grisham looked at his father as he said, "I can't imagine how your family would fare without you. We can't afford for either of you or anyone else, to be incapacitated."

Everyone around Rystole apologized to the speaker and when the man seemed content he said, "Now, curfew is going to set in soon. If you need a place to stay we are putting together a safe house in one of the empty houses inside the town walls. I understand if you don't want to travel back to the farm tonight with those beasts out there."

The last thing that Rystole wanted to do after Grisham's scolding was participate in his curfew. Unfortunately, his father agreed to take the speaker up on his offer of the spare house.

It was the right thing to do for the family as a whole, and the town would likely need the extra hands in the morning.

Eight

The next few days were chaotic as the town began its reinforcement process to protect itself from future slug attacks. Every night the colonists consolidated themselves to only a few houses with volunteer guards taking watches a few hours at a time.

During the days Rystole went out to various farms to help families. They always traveled in a group hoping that it would protect them from a slug attack.

Rystole didn't think numbers would matter if facing the slugs again. But at least in a large group there'd be time to flee or carry the bodies home.

School was still required by Speaker Grisham. He insisted that knowledge about the technologies used was absolutely necessary or else they could lose contact with the Central System in a few generations.

Rystole wasn't convinced that knowledge of how to communicate was necessary if there was an army of slugs that could make them all unconscious and useless to the Central System. But the speaker never asked his opinion. So he silently cut class to help the traveling ranchers. None seemed to mind his truancy or having a well-experienced young man helping out.

Rystole occasionally had the chance to sneak into the town hall. Getting past Grisham, who was always eager to shoo him out of the building, was difficult but not impossible.

He often found Bert working on documentation for the weapon he'd created. Sending it out to the Central System was of utmost importance, according to the speaker.

Otherwise, Rystoled knew he could find his friend with Doctor Yu.

On those days both of them would have their heads down analyzing the living slug that crawled around in a sealed glass tank.

There was never a way for Rystole to get in a word or question. He hardly had time to catch up and understand what they were studying.

So when Rystole went to visit after dinner one night and he found the two of them hovering over the captured slug's tank and a new contraption in Bert's hand he was interested but unhopeful he'd get any answers.

"What are y'all doing?" Rystole asked.

It startled both Bert and Dr. Yu and they immediately made a hand gesture indicating he should be quiet.

Rystole approached the wheeled table that held the slug's glass tank. The brown blob crept around the tank apparently recovered from whatever damage the gun had done on the night of the invasion.

The edges of its body moved like waves on a lake. The motion propelled it forward and left a thin layer of slime behind it.

Based on the cloudy residue on the glass it seemed like this slug had covered most of the walls and floor in the goop leaving a dried mess behind.

The more interesting, and less disgusting, object in the room was the new contraption Bert held. It was a mishmash of radio dials and antennas along with some electronic parts Rystole recognized from the gun, specifically the purple submitter crystal embedded in the center of the circuit board.

Bert's hands moved constantly but carefully over the device as he tweaked dials and stretched wires.

With one of Bert's changes, the device's microphone erupted with static.

Dr. Yu and Bert became visibly excited leaving Rystole confused. It was as if he'd just walked into a dining room to find the table attached to the ceiling and everyone centered around it waiting for him to begin the meal.

"Why's there static?" Rystole asked.

With the crystal in the center, Rystole assumed this design was based on a submitter radio. And those radios didn't get static like old analog ones.

The pair ignored his question and continued to adjust the radio. He watched Bert's hands move delicately across the dials as he adjusted parts of the contraption. And then out of nowhere, the static stopped.

"Undo it, undo it!" the doctor said frantically.

Bert was already retracing his steps. He had to reverse more than one of the tweaks he'd made to the dials but eventually the static returned.

"What's sending that?" Rystole asked. A submatter radio would only play static if something was transmitting it. He had a guess but he wasn't sure wanted to be right.

"From what we can tell, it's coming from the slug," Bert said. His face didn't reveal that he was making a joke. Even if it was sometimes hard to tell with Bert.

"Yeah right," Rystole said. "It's more likely you busted something in there and it's messing with the speaker."

"That's what I said," the doctor replied. "But then I did this."

The doctor took a scalpel off the operating table and carefully lifted the heavy glass lid off of the slug's tank.

He sliced at the slug with a gloved hand. As he cut through the slug's skin the static on the radio became less chaotic and organized itself into a chorus of chilling screams.

The doctor stopped and the static returned. The slug's skin that the doctor cut through sealed as if he'd never cut it.

"It's—" Rystole found a chair and sat down. "That's not possible."

The pair shrugged as if they couldn't disagree.

"Is it a robot or an android or something?" Rystole asked.

Rystole would sooner believe that rogue scientists in the Central System built these before he believed the ridiculous alternative. There was no way these primitive slugs could transmit on humanity's radio frequencies.

"Based on what I dissected," the doctor said, "these slugs are biological. There are no DNA markers indicating it's genetically manufactured. And if there's a chip in there it's too small for me to find."

Bert was quiet on the matter. He seemed to be processing something on his own and making notes on the settings of his circuit as it continued to play frustrating static in the background.

Rystole tapped his foot in the chair. He was having a hard time getting a grip on the situation. "Are there any other creatures that can—"

He was cut off by the sound of someone asking "Why's there static?"

Then the doctor said, "Undo it, undo it."

The trio looked around among themselves seeing no one else in the room.

Rystole's stomach dropped as he realized the static had stopped.

"It's using the radio," Bert finally said. The words sounded like they were being dragged out of him.

"That is correct. We are using the radio," and the voice sounded like a room full of people speaking in tandem.

"No. This is a prank," Rystole said. "Don't you two have anything better to do?"

As he looked at the doctor and his friend their expressions showed they were as terrified as him.

"This is not a prank," the chorus of voices replied.

Rystole got out of the chair and approached the glass tank. Once he got close enough he could tell the voice came from the radio.

"We are the slug," it said. The voices coming out of the radio were eerie. They made him uncomfortable.

"Turn it off," Rystole pleaded.

"That's not going to stop us from hearing you," the chorus replied. "Please. Speak with us."

The voices were almost singing. It would've been soothing from anything but an alien killer.

"Why would we?" Rystole said. "You've done nothing but attack us."

Before Rystole could get on a roll with a rant describing his mother and the other towns folk the slugs had hurt Dr. Yu rested his hand on Rystole's shoulder.

"Let's hear them out," the doctor said.

"Thank you," the chorus said. "We only attacked because you attacked first. Since you first arrived here we've been plagued by interference and our reach has been forced to dwindle."

"Bert and I only hunted you after you attacked my mother," Rystole corrected the slug.

"You've been hurting us far longer," the chorus said. "Although it seems you didn't notice. There has been interference in our—" static cut them off "—and it has been hard to maintain the sustenance needed."

"When we shot you with the gun in the forest, is that the interference you're talking about?" Bert asked.

"I have not been able to reconnect with the limb you approached in the forest yet," the voices replied.

"What do you mean reconnect?" Dr. Yu asked, glancing over at the case the dissected slug was stored in.

"We are connected to all slugs. Each slug contributes to the tribe and all slugs are controlled together."

"Do you have a queen?" Dr. Yu asked.

"We have no ruler, our tribe is vast and all are equal. But your interference has made it difficult to connect with some of our members."

"How many members do you have in your tribe?" The doctor asked.

Rystole was unnerved seeing one of the most intelligent men on the planet take this entire conversation seriously. It still felt unreal to Rystole, he was talking to a genuinely alien species. One that they had no defense against and could knock them out with a touch.

"We once had connections to enough limbs that we wrapped around the world."

"How did you discover submatter communication?" Bert asked.

Rystole was glad his friend asked the question that burned in Rystole's mind because as far as anyone had seen the slugs had no technology.   .

There was a pause before the chorus of voices responded, "We have always connected in this way. Figuring out how to connect with you has been harder. At first, it was like connecting with a tree. Impossible.

But after we were attacked in the forest we found that you did have this open connection. But I will say communicating with you is slow and uncomfortable."

"How do you speak Common Tongue," Rystole asked unsure how it knew the language of the Central System.

"We have listened intently for years trying to communicate. We felt your vibrations and realized it was how you connect with others of your tribe."

"Pretty smart for a bug," Rystole said with a grunt.

"Our intelligence comes from our numbers, not our individuals. Without connection to the whole, a slug will become unpredictable, blind, and eventually die after a few months without access to sustenance."

"You've injured our people. Are you aware of this?" Dr. Yu asked.

"We are. We are sorry. But it was the only way we knew of to communicate what you were doing to us. We needed your attention."

"So they're no better than my little brother who punches people for attention," Rystole said, disgusted.

"We weren't doing much better," Bert pointed out, "we killed a sentient being without knowing it."

"More like dismembering one," the chorus of voices interjected. "We suspected we would not be able to reconnect with that limb ever again."

"I'm sorry," Bert said and he sounded more genuine than Rystole felt. But Bert hadn't lost his mom to the beasts.

"We did not attack with the intent to kill," the chorus continued. "We only wanted to disconnect you like you disconnected us."

Rystole hated the idea that he was merely disconnected from his mother. It was too simple. Too impersonal. Like he'd simply hung up the radio. She wasn't living a life independently without him, she was unresponsive and in a coma.

"We have a way to reconnect you," the chorus continued, "but we need you to stop the interference."

"What's causing the interference?" Rystole asked.

"It's the comms tower," Bert answered. His tone was familiar, it was the same voice he used when in school when he realized the right answer *after* turning in a test.

"It can't be," Rystole protested. "They're slugs, they don't have any advanced technology like this."

"Evolution will do some tricky things," Yu explained, "like insects attracted to old incandescent light bulbs."

"There's not actually any electronics at the heart of the submatter communications systems," Bert explained. "All the electronics are used to translate data we understand to the crystal. The crystal itself is just a complex set of chemicals that resonate with other submatter crystals."

"But we'd be able to find a crystal in the slug we dissected and we didn't," Rystole said as if he was the only one bringing logic to this conversation.

"I found a lot of things I didn't understand," Yu said, "and if it's complex chemicals there could be a chance it's not solid like a crystal but more organic, like a spleen."

"The organ we use to connect to others of our kind is our," static cut in, "gland and it's located in the back left quadrant about two-thirds of the way towards our rear."

Yu made a note on his hand terminal and then asked, "The ability to reseal your skin which gland manages—"

Rystole cut the doctor off. There were more important things to discuss. "You said there's a way to reconnect us with those you've attacked?" Rystole asked.

"We can generate a compound that will reverse the effects of the original neurotoxin," the chorus of voices explained. "Each one is uniquely tailored to its subject, but we would be willing to reconnect you with one as a sign of good faith. Simply place this slug on the body of one of the patients you want reconnected and we'll do the rest."

The group was hesitant and Dr. Yu asked several questions mostly focused on how to safely transport the slug without getting knocked out himself.

Once the doctor was comfortable they wheeled the table that held the glass tank to the infirmary. The doctor carefully moved the slug from the case onto Mr. Montgomery. Slowly the man came back to consciousness.

Rystole stood next to his mother holding her unresponsive hand. He wished Dr. Yu would wake her up. But Montgomery had been out the longest and Yu wasn't taking input on how to do his job.

But now they had a cure for the comas. They'd just need to convince the town to take the submatter comms tower offline. Which should be an easy bargain since the town as a whole didn't use it that often.

Nine

Rystole tapped his foot as he sat in the front row of the auditorium for the second time in just as many town hall meetings. He rarely sat in the front row, often he showed up late and sat in the back.

But today Dr. Yu was going to address the colony, or at least those still conscious, about their findings of the slug.

Rystole hoped that this announcement went his way. Unlike the last.

Most of the people in the room seemed nervous as well. There was whispered talk instead of the usual dull thrum of chatter from people who hadn't seen each other for weeks.

But the colony had been in close quarters lately. Additionally, the memory of slugs invading the last town hall meeting was fresh in everyone's mind, causing people to be on edge to return.

Dr. Yu sat on stage in a row of mostly empty printed chairs. Chairs meant for those who were to speak tonight. But there wasn't much to talk about. Routine bureaucracy, traditional announcements, and weather events felt pointless after the last slug attack.

Yu wore his white coat and wrinkled khaki slacks. The man was rubbing the back of his left hand with his right thumb rhythmically.

Rystole hoped that it wasn't nerves. He hoped the man on stage could make a case for the slugs. At a minimum make a case for saving his patients.

Speaker Grisham kicked off the meeting with a long rambling of the same mundane announcements he always did. He brought up the effectiveness of the curfew and the delays of upcoming holiday events.

He eventually passed the podium off to Dr. Yu. Which was when Rystole was able to confirm that the incessant rubbing was, in fact, nerves.

"Thank you, Speaker," Dr. Yu said into the microphone. His voice wavered as he spoke and he followed the gratitude with a few ums seemingly hesitant to get started.

"I'd like to reiterate my gratitude to everyone who has worked to reinforce our town's defenses over the past week. Everyone has a key role to play in our engagement with the slugs.

"I'd like to specifically thank Mr. Morris for his tireless research," the doctor gestured to Bert who was sitting in the front row next to Rystole. "I'm proud to announce that we are now able to establish communication with the slug creatures. We believe—"

The doctor tried to continue but the audience clamored with excitement. Despite the amplification of the microphone, Yu stood no chance with every person trying to talk over their neighbors.

A flurry of questions was slung at Dr. Yu.

"Where are we with negotiations?"

"Why are we negotiating at all?"

"Have they revealed any tactical weaknesses?"

"What's their purpose of attacking us?"

The doctor answered the questions as best he could. It was clear to Rystole that the crowd was barking up the wrong tree. And each question Dr. Yu answered seemed to stem two more.

Speaker Grisham, who seemed as taken back as everyone else, eventually walked up to the podium and waved his hands to calm the crowd down.

Once their questions quit being answered they quit asking.

"Let us hear what Dr. Yu has to say," Grisham said. "I'm sure he will answer your questions in the process." The Speaker relinquished the microphone over to Yu again.

Rystole was amazed at how crowd control was almost entirely unlike herding buffcows. He gained a little bit better understanding of why Dr. Yu was nervous. And didn't relish the job the doctor or speaker had.

"From our communications with them we have learned that they are peaceful and are willing to work with us—"

The crowd responded to this with a mix of loud incredulity, sarcastic remarks, and blatant denial.

The Speaker stood up to his chair and repeated his arm waiving but didn't need to take the podium to calm them down again.

"The slug we've captured has promised to give us an antidote for the citizens that are in a coma in exchange for turning off the submatter radio tower," Dr. Yu said.

The crowd murmured. Seeming to weigh the options among each other.

Rystole was uninterested in the murmuring. The speaker had stood up at Dr. Yu's statement and begun exchanging words with the doctor.

The speaker's voice was hushed, or at least quiet enough that the microphone didn't pick it up. And Rystole's front-row seat wasn't close enough to overhear them.

But the results of his words were clear on Dr. Yu's face. He looked like a boy who'd just been caught interrupting a shuttle's lift-off because he thought he might have left his teddy bear onboard.

The doctor sat down in the row of empty seats as the speaker took the podium over.

"As you are all aware, this is not a viable solution," Grisham announced over the murmuring of the crowd. "The submatter satellite is one of the most important pieces of equipment we have on this colony and without it we'd be cut off from the Central System."

The townsfolk had quieted completely by this point.

"We don't know the intentions or intelligence of this species and this could be a further ruse to attack while we're cut off. We're all aware of the hostility they've shown us over the past months and we have no reason to trust them now."

"But we've talked with them," Rystole blurted out at the speaker. "They're intelligent. And they've already cured Mr. Montgomery,"

The speaker was only caught off guard for a second. "If they are intelligent then they knew what they were doing," Grisham replied to Rystole without addressing him directly. "Their actions were immoral and malicious. And we have no reason to trust them or negotiate with them."

"We don't even use the—" Rystole started, but the speaker raised his voice and the microphone's amplification overran Rystole's protests.

"Mr. Morris has also devised a way to eliminate the slugs in a way that we were not previously capable of. I've sent his design to the Central System's engineering department and we expect a printable design to arrive within the month.

"I'll remind everyone that a Central System minister is in transit to judge the situation and determine the long-term fate of these slugs.

Until then we will continue with the curfew efforts that have been effective up to this point."

Rystole spat a few protests at the speaker, and a few others in the crowd seemed to agree with him.

Despite this, the speaker turned off the microphone and exited the stage. Dr. Yu followed him like a hesitant dog on a leash.

Without Speaker Grisham, the meeting was over without much room for debate.

Ten

Rystole sat on the porch of his family's empty timber frame home. The boards squeaked as he leaned back and forth in the rocking chair. The motion was uneven and hesitant from the rough boards underneath and the hand-carved slope of the chair's rocker feet.

His father had carved it when his youngest sister was born. He remembered his mother holding her, and later his youngest brother Harry, in it to get her to fall asleep.

The sun had all but set. The evening was cool but not chilly. Bugs chirped in the grass and the buffcows hemmed and hawed in their pen getting comfortable for the evening. Barley fields that were painted orange and yellow in midday sun looked blue and purple thanks to the planet's first moon already being in the sky.

The house was empty. His mother was in the infirmary and the rest of his family was safe inside of the town's walls.

Where he was supposed to be.

Safe from the slugs.

Rystole didn't feel like the slugs were much of a threat anymore. Not with Grisham undermining Rystole and the colony's progress at every point.

The colony's speaker, and the ways he thwarted Rystole, used to remind the boy of a vice principal character in a classic comedy movie he watched on Feldman's station. The vice principal would chase after this wily student to try to get him to attend class or prove the boy was up to something devious.

Tonight, and Rystole expected for the foreseeable future, Grisham felt like he was the villain of a space station noir film. One who was always one step ahead of the detective. Putting him in a worse position every other scene.

Rystole noticed someone on the horizon. A bright white flashlight wagged back and forth. Whoever held it was approaching the house.

Probably yet another authority figure, out to bring him to justice.

Or at least drag him to a concrete bedroom built by a machine, not a family.

Rystole rocked defiantly in his chair. The boards creaked under him. The nails that he'd handed to his dad when they were building the place held the deck together.

Which was more than Rystole could say for the rest of the life they'd built here.

The flashlight-carrying traveler was in fact another authority figure: Rystole's father.

The man stood at the base of the porch's two steps and leaned on the post that held the roof up.

"Mind if I join you?" He asked.

Rystole shrugged at the dumb question. The porch belonged to his father just as much as Rystole. Hell, technically more since he was the adult.

His father flipped the flashlight off. There was just enough light in the sky to navigate the familiar porch.

The man sat in an old printed chair. One they'd brought out from town when they were constructing the house. They left it on the porch since it could withstand the elements.

"Heard about the town hall meeting," his father said. He kicked his feet onto the low railing. It was only high enough to keep the toddlers from falling off the platform. To everyone else, the half-meter fall was merely a large step.

The creaking of Rystole's rocking chair was the only reply his father received.

"Sounds like Dr. Yu and the speaker have some ideas of how to make things better."

"Not that it's going to get us very far."

"We're in a better spot than we were yesterday. Better off than ever before."

"Mom's still—" Rystole's voice caught, "—not here."

"Dr. Yu and Speaker are smart people and they got where they were because they care about the colony. We wouldn't put people in charge that didn't."

"*I* didn't put anyone in charge. Neither did you. They were appointed by some bureaucrat who saw that their application fit the job's specifications."

Grisham was just a peg that fit in a hole. And after tonight it was clear Yu was just an automaton following orders.

"They're here. They know us. They care. They have skin in the game. They're not some bureaucrat a few dozen jumps away."

"They might as well be," Rystole said. He kicked his feet up on the banister and stopped his rocking. "We've got an answer sitting right in front of us. But they're not willing to do anything about it."

"There are countless things Grisham has to consider with this decision. He can't just go promising everyone their family members back on the statement of an, up to now, aggressive alien slug."

"He barely heard Dr. Yu out. Didn't seem like he was taking *countless things* into consideration."

"Your great-grandmother was religious," his father said, meandering and detouring from the conversation at hand.

Rystole hated it when he did this.

"She was Christian, probably. She always said 'God works in mysterious ways' whenever something bad happened."

Rystole kicked back into the chair. Let it rock slowly until it loses its momentum. The creaking sound didn't cut his father off.

"I never found it particularly satisfying," his father said, more reminiscent than frustrated. "Felt like it was biased towards hindsight rather than genuine fact."

"Yeah and what? Now Grisham's god?" Rystole asked. The question was seething and sarcastic.

"No. More that I finally think I understand why she said it. It's because there's nothing better to say in moments like this."

His father gave Rystole a subtle grin like he'd told a joke and expected Rystole to burst out in laughter once the punchline landed.

Rystole wanted to burst out in a dozen curses.

"We have a solution. We have a cure." Rystole was almost shouting as he spoke. It echoed through the quiet night. "Montgomery is up. Mom could be here tomorrow. The slugs could be out of our hair. I can't believe anyone who cares about the colony is willing to ignore such an obvious solution."

"The Central System has protocols for handling intelligent extraterrestrials who have acted aggressively against us.

"But the slugs want to help now."

Rystole heard that he sounded like Juniper whining about being a sore loser. Hated himself for it. Didn't know how to stop.

"They explained why they were doing it," Rystole continued. "They're willing to stop if we agree to take down the tower. It's so simple. We don't use the thing!"

"Then it sounds like we have the means to eventually heal mom and all the others that were hurt." His father was frustratingly calm as he spoke. "This isn't a negotiation that the Speaker, or Dr. Yu, can handle out of process or on their own—"

"She could be back tomorrow!" A buffcow groaned from its pen startled by Rystole's shout.

"No one wants your mother back as much as I do," his father said. "You kids change and grow so much every day. And I hate that she's missing it."

"Then we do something to fix it." Rystole no longer sounded like his whining sister and he was glad about it.

"No Rye. We don't." It was a suggestion, not a command. "We can't rush the barley, we can't rush a pie, and we can't rush the herd without starting a stampede. So, we wait."

His father stood up and rubbed his hands together to fight off the chilly night air.

"I'm headed back to town. Stay here if you want. The herd will appreciate not having to wait 'til the pack of ranchers make their way out here."

Rystole crinkled his nose in frustration and avoided looking up at his father.

"But I want a hug before I go," his father said.

The man tugged on his son's hands. The rocking chair tipped forward betraying Rystole and he fell out of it and onto his feet.

His father wrapped his arms around Rystole and squeezed him tight.

There once was a time when his father would have picked him up while hugging. But now Rystole was nearly the same height and a good ten kilos of muscle heavier than his lean father.

Rystole had to settle for wrapping his arms around his dad and burring his chilly nose into the man's shoulder.

Eleven

Night had washed over the entire settlement. The second moon had risen in the sky, a waxing crescent. The first one had set hours ago, as Rystole had made his way into town.

It was strange to see Dale Cannon from this angle. He remembered looking down on the planet from orbit. It was impossible to see the settlement with the naked eye but an enhanced video feed showed the colonists where they were landing.

Back then it'd been a ready-made town built by large concrete printing rovers that'd been sent ahead of the colonists. The town followed a grid pattern with the town hall in the center and tall walls in an oval shape around it.

Back then the submatter radio tower hadn't even been erected next to the town hall. The colonists had done that themselves in the first weeks.

Looking through the metal grate that Rystole stood on he was closer than the satellite feed. And the town had changed significantly.

A few buildings were missing in the grid system, well-trodden streets ran through them for convenience. Signs were posted on the road and a few wooden extensions had been added to the premanu-factured concrete houses.

But the biggest difference Rystole noticed was how easy it'd be to fall off the submatter radio tower. You didn't get that sensation from looking at a satellite image.

No one would find him until morning. Who knows if they'd be able to identify him once he hit the ground.

But it wouldn't be hard to figure out who it was. There was only one person bold enough to climb up the submatter radio tower in the middle of the night. Only one person was willing to do what needed to be done.

Rystole found a climbing harness and rope at the bottom of the tower in a locker with no lock on it. The belt fit fine but the straps around his legs were a bit tight. Two carabiners that were attached to the harness let him clip into a safety line when he climbed up the metal rungs embedded into the tower to form a ladder.

A belay device, made up of a complicated set of pulleys, would let him lower himself on the rope if he needed to. But he'd prefer to just climb the ladder down. It'd be slower but safer.

The only other thing he carried up here was a bag of tools he'd scrounged from the ranch. A drill, screwdriver, an array of wrenches and screwdrivers.

At the bottom was a hammer. In case things came to that.

He didn't know what he'd run into up here. The colony's technician manual that they studied in school was lacking in details when it came to the innards of the radio.

Luckily he didn't have to understand the radio to know how to break it. He just hoped he didn't do anything irreversible.

A cool breeze passed by him but it felt refreshing on his face. He was wearing a tan canvas jacket with a thick lining on the inside. It was nice for the walk into town but after climbing all the way up here he was sweating and warm.

The submatter radio equipment was stored in a metal cylinder cabinet that started at about Rystole's knee and stopped at his chest.

Above the cabinet, a pole extended another two meters with a horizontal ladder-like antenna at the top. A flashing red light blinked just under it, for if, or when, people started flying vehicles around this planet.

The cabinet itself was, surprisingly, locked with a circular padlock. Rystole was surprised considering security on the colony was pretty relaxed. With only a few hundred people and an interdependence on each other for survival, it wasn't advantageous to steal from your neighbor and betray their trust.

And then there was Rystole who was about to betray the trust of every one of those citizens. Maybe those who had family members in comas would be sympathetic to his cause. Maybe a few more could empathize with him. But he didn't expect to be winning any popularity contests for a while after this.

He didn't care.

He wanted his mother conscious again.

Rystole pulled the drill out of his tool bag and went to work on the lock. It didn't take long, the security was only there to keep unmotivated people out. And right now that didn't include Rystole.

Inside of the metal cabinet, embedded in a poster-sized circuit board, the submatter crystal glowed purple. This crystal was bigger than any that Rystole had seen.

It was about the size of Juniper's head. Certainly, it was larger than the ones Bert had worked with to make the gun or the translation radio.

He didn't want to touch it. He didn't want to do anything irreparable.

Rystole pulled out a pair of wire cutters and started snipping the green, white, and black power lines that were hooked into the bottom of the circuit board. Sparks flew as he cut into the first two. It startled him but didn't stop him.

At least without power removed he wouldn't fry anything on the circuit board.

He stared at the board trying to decide what to remove next.

A siren went off.

Rystole jumped then grabbed onto the open door of the cabinet to steady himself.

The pulsing of the sirens disturbed the once-quiet night.

They'd caught onto him. He wouldn't be able to do anything else to the radio. It'd be fixed by morning.

Looking down dot-sized people came out of their house to look around. A few guards, volunteer ranchers, that were posted started running towards the tower.

Rystole was busted.

He had no time to climb the ladder. They'd surely spot him during his slow descent.

He looped the rope around the sturdy ladder rung and fed the tail ends of the rope through the belay device following the instructions engraved into it.

If he wanted a chance at escape he'd have to quickly lower himself down. And even then he might not be fast enough.

Holding onto the top ladder rung with both hands Rystole took a deep breath and sat back in the harness.

When it was clear the rope and belay device were capable of holding him he let go of the ladder.

Using the lever of the belay device he lowered himself as fast as he could stand without his stomach coming out of his throat.

Cold night air rushed through his hair and up his jacket. It didn't stop his nervous sweating.

More people were rushing to the tower. He lowered himself as quickly as he could get away with. Strangely no one seemed to be looking up or circling around it. There might be a chance to escape.

When Rystole's boots finally touched the ground there was not a ring of volunteer guards surrounding him. Grisham hadn't been roused from bed to figure out what was going on.

Rystole was lucky. For now.

He slipped out of the harness but left it all hanging there. It was clear that someone'd messed with the tower. No point in hiding the evidence and delaying his escape.

There was one thing worth doing to delay his escape.

Rystole slipped into the town hall. The alarms had caused the doors to unlock. It was the shelter location for situations when the alarms went off.

Rystole made his way towards the infirmary. He wanted to use the slug that was in there to heal his mother before he slipped out of the town.

He entered the infirmary and was shocked by who he found in there.

A half dozen people, including his mother, lay in beds unconscious. In the center of the room, next to the glass tank that held the captured slug, stood Bert. He was playing with the translation radio.

"What are you doing here?" Rystole asked.

"What are either of you doing here?" Dr. Yu asked from behind Rystole.

The doctor wore a wrinkled lab coat and an oversized sweater under it and held a radio in his hand that was full of garbled chatter from panicked townsfolk.

The doctor must have heard Rystole's heavy boots in the hallway.

"Hay for brains shut off the radio tower setting off all the alarms," Bert said. "I'm here to make sure the slugs make good on their end of the bargain."

"How'd you know I—" Rystole started to ask.

"The alarms are going off because the slugs are attacking the town," Dr. Yu said.

"Oh," Bert said sounding a little shocked and very concerned.

"Why are they attacking?" Rystole asked.

That wasn't what was supposed to happen. The beasts were supposed to cure his mom not hit them while they couldn't call for help.

The slugs had betrayed them. And Rystole had been complicit in the scheme.

"We are here," the chorus of voices said from Bert's radio, "to 'make good on our end of the bargain,' as you say."

A gunshot rang out through the halls and over the radio. Rystole shivered. If someone was resorting to firearms it'd be bad.

"Where's that boy's gun?" Grisham said over the radio. "The one I have isn't working on them."

"They're in the auditorium!" someone else said.

"That's where everyone's sheltering," Bert said.

"It's touching my leg. Elder's please," someone pleaded.

"I touched one, I'm not unconscious," another voice announced.

"We mean you no harm," the chorus of voices said. "Did you not tell your limbs we were coming?"

"I thought I could use the one in the tank," Rystole said.

"That limb of ours does not have the resources. It has not eaten to replenish itself."

"You haven't fed it?" Rystole asked.

"I didn't know what it ate," Dr. Yu said a little ashamed.

"You could've asked," Bert said gesturing to the radio in his hand.

"Communication is not your species' strong suit is it?" the chorus of voices asked.

Before any of the humans could reply slugs entered the infirmary.

At first, it was one. Then a half dozen. But in a matter of seconds, the entire floor was covered with the goopy beasts.

Some crawled up the tables. Others crawled on the medical equipment or the walls.

They brushed past the tops of Rystole's boots. As more flowed in he could feel them brush against his leg despite the thick canvas of his pants.

They were squishy and slimy and left trails of goop on the walls. The room was flooding with them soon the pile of slugs would be up to Rystole's waist.

The slugs brushed past his hand. Despite the touch being harmless he jerked away in shock.

He waded through the tide of slugs towards his mother's bed. Patients were waking up with gasps and screaming in shock at the slugs.

Dr. Yu tried to reassure his patients over the chaos of the radio, the beeping medical equipment, and the screaming patients. His words had little effect.

A slug crawled across his mother's arm. Rystole reached for her hand. The pool of slugs seemed to push him towards her faster.

His mother gasped awake as he clasped his hand around hers. She looked at him panicked like she was facing down a buffbull.

"It's okay," Rystole reassured her, resting his hand on her arm. "Everything's okay."

The tide of slugs receded from the room slipping out thin cracks in windows, air vents, and the hallway. They disappeared faster than they entered.

In a moment they were all gone. Only a thin residue of slick slime covered the floor to prove they'd been there.

His mother and every other patient in the room had a dozen questions. Before Rystole or Dr. Yu could answer them Grisham stood in the doorway.

Two ranchers stood behind him. Grisham had a blocky pistol in his hand.

"Rystole Whitman," the town's speaker said, "you're under arrest."

Twelve

Rystole and Bert sat in the locked town hall office they'd called home for the past week. It was the best the town could do for a jail and Grisham was dead set on not letting the boys roam free in the town.

Rystole's father often visited on his lunch break and gave his son updates about how his mother was doing.

All the news was good, it seemed like she was already back to her old chores on the ranch. She occasionally came to visit in the evenings. The time was nice but not nearly as long as Rystole wished it could be.

However, their stay in this small office would end today. One way or another. The Minister from the Central System had landed last night.

They would make a judgment on whether or not Rystole and Bert would be deported and if the submatter radio would have to go back up.

It'd stayed down, for some reason. Rystole had no idea why and worried he'd done more damage than he meant to.

Based on his description of the wires he'd cut Bert assured him that was unlikely the radio was irreparable. But that didn't stop the engineer from coming up with theories of how Rystole could've messed up.

Which didn't ease Rystole's concerns.

A man Rystole didn't recognize came in, that alone was a clue he was from the Central System. The long white robes of his position as a minister only further gave him away.

He had dark hair a sharp chin and hazel eyes that seemed compassionate for someone who had to make so many harsh judgments across so many planets.

The minister unlocked the office door and asked the boys to come with him. He led them down the hall to a small office that was almost identical to the one they'd just spent a week in.

This one had three plastic seats and a wooden table in the center. Some crates were piled in the corner of the room.

The minister shuffled some files on a portable terminal he had set up before addressing the boys.

"I'm Minister Mayhew," the man said. "And I've been told you two are responsible for the events of last week."

"He's not. I am." Rystole said.

"No," Bert protested. "I helped a little. If anything I'm the mastermind. He's just a farm boy caught up in my plans."

The minister rolled his eyes as if he'd seen this conversation play out a dozen times before.

"Look, neither of you are in trouble. I'm not going to be deporting you to some black-site prison facility or even off this planet. If anything, with your design Mr. Morris I should be trying to recruit you to do CS R&D. Your weapon, and more importantly, the translation radio you designed, will be helpful on this planet and others like it."

"Thank you," Bert said, but not as thrilled as expected.

"So if we're not in trouble, what are you going to do?" Rystole asked still nervous to get the the point. "Did you bring a militia and more weapons?"

"There's an improved version of Mr. Morris' design that we can manufacture here. I brought a few commandos. In case you needed help dealing with the immediate threat. They would train you colonists long term... but after the situation last week I'm not sure that's going to work out."

"What do you mean?" Bert asked.

"I've watched the footage of the entire..." the minister paused looking for the right word, couldn't find one then settled on, "event. How many slugs do you think you saw in the infirmary?"

"Maybe a thousand?" Rystole replied.

"I've done the calculations a few times in the past week," Bert replied. "If they filled the infirmary up to our waist and the slugs are just under liter each it'd be something like 50 thousand slugs in that room alone."

"The entire town hall was filled like that room," the minister said. "And footage shows the entire town square and streets were flooded with a quarter meter layer of them. The only safe place was the houses, and I think that was just because they weren't interested in them."

"That's," Rystole paused to fathom how many that was, "so many."

"They aren't dumb, based on the transcripts. You'll agree with that, no?"

"We agree," Bert said on behalf of them both.

"They were trying to show us their true strength. And I'm unwilling to believe that was their entire colony. I would certainly leave a reserve of people if I was doing an operation like that. If only to avoid tipping my hand."

"The slugs we spoke to said they wrapped all around the planet," Rystole added.

"Yes," the minister seemed concerned but not displeased. "I worry this was just the numbers they could mobilize in the short amount of time the tower was down."

He paused to let that sink in with the boys.

"We couldn't kill them with your weapons if we tried," Mayhew finally said. "They'd put everyone in a comma in an instant. Or worse."

"Which is why the tower hasn't been turned on again?" Bert concluded.

"Exactly," the minister said. "We're beginning plans to set up a satellite with a submatter radio in orbit. For now, my ship is working as a relay. You're not completely cut off but you'll have to use traditional means to access my ship and you'll be cut off while it's on the far side of the planet."

"So we can live in harmony with them?" Rystole asked, shocked that that could even be a possibility.

The minister shrugged. "They have the numbers. But humanity needs this planet to be a hub to continue its expansion into the stars. That's still a generation or two away but it's coming."

"And a hub can't run efficiently with an orbital submatter radio," Bert pointed out.

The minister nodded his head. "To be frank, if you hadn't established communications we would have just designed a toxin, or something, to wipe them out. But, the Elders aren't keen on wiping out sapient life. It sets a bad precedent. So, you two have made my job a lot harder."

"Can we relocate them?" Rystole asked.

"It's a step up from genocide," the minister said. "But we'd have to find, or make, a planet that will hold them. There's no simple solution to this."

"Yeah and Speaker Grisham isn't going to do anything more complicated than genocide," Rystole said, but it felt harsher than he meant it to.

"I can't speak to that," the minister said. "But he has stepped down as speaker and will be leaving this colony. Along with a few other families unwilling to live on a planet with so many, once hostile, creatures."

"So, who's in charge?" Bert asked.

"For now I am interim speaker. Although I will the reviewing applications for a new speaker."

"You could apply," Bert said, nudging Rystole's arm.

Rystole gave a half-hearted grin. It was often difficult to tell when his friend was being serious.

"I can't honestly recommend a career in politics any more than a butcher can recommend sausages," the minister said with a shrug. "You would have to learn a thing or two about following procedures and not jumping immediately into action."

"I'll think about it," Rystole said, uneager to abandon a trait that'd served him well so recently.

Right now he was only interested in returning to the ranch and seeing his family in their home. Luckily, after a few more questions the minister let them go.

Bert headed to his house, the two friends had spent enough quality time together over the past week of being locked up.

Rystole passed under the tall concrete walls of the town and headed back to the farm. The day was cool, fall was here. Tall black storm clouds hung in the horizon, fall thunderstorms would be here soon.

Rystole began to think of the work that needed to be done on the farm to close out summer. Then about how he was glad to be able to stay on Dale Cannon, keep it his home. It was far more familiar and comfortable than the distant Feldman's station.

And he was more than willing to share the planet with the slugs. He didn't know how many other colonists would agree with that view and how many would be leaving with Grisham.

But his thoughts were interrupted by dozens of brown spots moving across the dirt path and in the tall grass along its edge.

There were slugs everywhere. No longer needing to hide from the humans.

Rystole kneeled next to one at the edge of the path. It was munching on a blade of grass. He hesitantly ran a knuckle down the slug's back.

The slug's skin was gooey but harmless. The slug arched its back pressing against Rystole's knuckle. The light brown rings on its back rotated with small waves.

He wasn't going to apply for speaker. At least not right now. It was far too demanding of a job and he could barely herd a pack of buffcows in a straight line, let alone a town of people.

Nonetheless, there was another herd on this planet. They hid underground.

And that herd needed someone willing to support and back them. Even willing to go outside of Central System's slow procedure sometimes.

After all this planet was their home first.

Also By Nicholas Licalsi

An Echo Through Time

T odd can travel through time and the multiverse. With a single focused breath, he can be any place and any time.

Instead, he relives the same day of high school over and over, knowing his sweetheart will die by lunch.

And there's nothing he can do to save her.

Equipped with time travel Todd rarely feels powerless, but his sweetheart's deaths make him question his place in the multiverse.

If you enjoy thrilling time travel stories An Echo Through Time will have you on the edge of your seat!

https://books2read.com/EchoThroughTime

Path of the Bearers and Other Stories

An AI with the potential to predict the future must uncover its creator's inexplicable disappearance. A scientist must reveal the limitations of his high profile project to while his investor takes them on a joyride through an asteroid field. A writer travels to a pocket dimension to find time to write, but something sinister follows.

Visit seedy space station bars, distant planets where dormant aliens rest. One wrong decision could ruin humanity's chances of surviving among the stars.

This book is your portal to explore the cosmos and beyond...
https://books2read.com/PathOfTheBearersAndOtherStories

Bleeding Rock

Mauve, a talented mechanic, always dreamed of leaving her satellite home. So she didn't think twice before signing up for a routine planetary survey.

Mauve awakes from the landing hanging upside down. Clearly something went wrong. She will need all her mechanical knowledge to get the mission back on track.

But the crash landing is only the start of her troubles.

With her AI assistant Mauve must use everything she discovers on this alien world to escape it.

If you enjoy science fiction exploration stories with elements of horror then you'll love Bleeding Rock!

https://books2read.com/BleedingRock

About the Author

Nicholas Licalsi was born and raised outside of Fort Worth, in the beautiful but backwards state of Texas. Growing up, he was fascinated with science fiction and fantasy. This interest led to pursuing a degree in engineering and participating in multiple robotics competitions. After a successful enough career in software development Nicholas spends his time trying to trick his overactive imagination into paying the bills while he satiates his dog's need to be pet.

You can connect with me at: https://stepintotheroad.com

Get updates about my upcoming books at: https://stepintoth eroad.com/signup

www.ingramcontent.com/pod-product-compliance
Lightning Source LLC
Chambersburg PA
CBHW022046170626
46808CB00003B/1379